The Night Rescue

The Secret Dinosaur
Book 4

N.S. Blackman

Text and illustrations copyright © 2015
N.S. Blackman

All Rights Reserved
Published by Dinosaur Books Ltd, London

www.dinosaurbooks.co.uk
Dinoteks™ Sonya McGilchrist

ISBN 978-0-9930105-6-9
British Library Cataloguing in Publication Data
A CIP catalogue record for this book is available from
the British Library
Printed and bound in Great Britain by TJ International Ltd

Dacky
Pteranodon Dinotek

Tyrannosaurus Rex Dinotek

Flame

Marlin
Homo Sapiens (juvenile)

Siggy
(or Comp?)

Troodon Dinotek

The Night Rescue
By N.S. Blackman

Protos

Centrosaurus Dinotek

Steg

Little Dragon
Meganeura Dinotek

Stegosaurus Dinotek

Now available in the **Dinoteks** series

The Secret Dinosaur – Giants Awake!
The Secret Dinosaur – Hunters Attack!
The Secret Dinosaur – Jurassic Adventure
The Secret Dinosaur – The Night Rescue

The Lost Dinosaur (for younger readers)

Visit www.dinoteks.com for the latest titles,
puzzles and activities featuring the Dinoteks

About the Dinoteks

Next time you go to a museum look out for the dusty old dinosaur that nobody else is interested in.

There's usually one.

Most people think it's just an old model – a relic left over from the days when such things weren't very realistic.

But if you know what to look for, and if you are really lucky, you might discover an amazing secret…

www.dinoteks.com

With best wishes to
Leo Pesce
Renzi Pesce
Pablo Ortega
and
Oscar Cloud
thanks for being so cool guys!

Chapter One

· ·

A Collector
of Rare Things

The house was dark. A pile of dirty dishes was spilling out of the kitchen sink and a trail of bread crumbs led from the table, up the stairs, to the bedroom door.

A glob of butter was stuck to the door handle. And inside the room Oliver Grubbler was sitting up in bed, eating egg sandwiches.

Grubbler used to be an important man. He used to be the manager of the museum. But then he lost his job.

And from that day until this he had done nothing except sit in bed and eat.

And eat.

And on this particular Thursday night it was egg sandwiches again. Big thick ones with chewy crusts.

Grubbler took another bite – CHOMP – then he stopped, and he stared.

"Wha…?!"

A pair of feet was dangling outside his window!

"How?! Who…?"

Boots! Just hanging there!

Grubbler blinked. His mouth hung open in astonishment and a piece of half-chewed sandwich slid down his chin.

****

The boots at the window began to move downwards.

Two yellow socks came into view. Then a pair of shiny, black waterproof trousers.

Two scrubbed hands, with gold rings on the fingers appeared.

And finally there was a face.

A woman was staring in at him.

She leaned forward and tapped on the glass with her fingernail – CLICKETY! CLICK! – and the nail scraped downwards – SKREEEK! SKREEEEEEEEK!

The horrible sound prompted Grubbler into action at last. He jumped up and ran to fling open the window.

"Who are you? Where did you come from? How are you *doing* that...?"

He peered into the evening gloom, trying to see how the woman was floating in the air.

But she ignored him.

"You look disgusting," she said. "Your face needs washing. Open the front door."

Then she was gone, dropping downwards out of view.

******

The woman was waiting on the doorstep. As Grubbler opened the door he caught a glimpse of a hook disappearing upwards on the end of a chain. He leaned forward to see more but the chain swung away into the dark.

"What is that?"

The woman ignored him and pushed into the hall.

"Grubbler! How long have you been wearing those pyjamas?"

Grubbler looked down at himself and noticed for the first time that his favourite yellow pyjamas were now a grimy grey. The only bit of yellow left was the dried-up egg yoke stuck to the one of the sleeves.

"I'm doing my washing tomorrow," he snorted. "Not that it's any of *your* business. And how did you know my name?"

"It is my business," answered the woman. "I can't work with people who are dirty."

Now she was walking ahead, into the kitchen.

"Eh? Wait a moment, who said I was working with you?"

"My name is Arangula Snidd," she replied. "And I want to talk to you about dinosaurs."

****

Dinosaurs. Or not dinosaurs exactly, Dino*teks* – the machine creatures that lived at the museum.

"What about them?" snorted Grubbler.

"I want them," she replied simply. "I am a collector of rare things."

11

Grubbler laughed.

"You're wasting your time."

But the woman just smiled.

"You think so?"

She cleared a space on the table, sweeping a heap of breadcrumbs onto the floor with her sleeve. Then she spread open a large sheet of paper. She leaned over it like an army commander poised over the map of a battle.

"I have a plan Grubbler. And I need your help."

Grubbler peered at the paper. It was covered in spidery writing, pictures, arrows and diagrams. Arangula Snidd pointed.

"Look. The Dinoteks have a weakness."

Grubbler looked. And he frowned.

"Weakness?" he muttered. "Hmmm… weakness… where's the weakness…"

"It's *here* Grubbler!"

She prodded the plan.

"Look! The Dinoteks are all powered by batteries, correct?"

"Yes but…"

"And batteries don't last forever do they?"

"No. Of course not. Well, not unless you re-charge them."

"Exactly!"

Her eyes sparkled at him.

"*That's* their weakness. We need to find out how the Dinoteks re-charge their batteries. Once we know that, we can stop them powering up. They'll freeze. And I can capture them."

Grubbler scratched his head.

"So what do you need me for?"

"Information," she replied. "Tell me everything you know about the creatures. And about the people protecting them – Professor Cogwell and the boy, Marlin."

Grubbler thought for a moment and picked at the dried egg on his sleeve.

"Maybe I will…" he said.

"I'll also need you to do some sneaking about," added Snidd. "And some stealing."

"Stealing?"

"Yes."

She folded away the plan.

"It will be fun," she said.

"Fun..."

Grubbler kept the scowl on his face.

He didn't want her to think that he was really interested – but he was. For the first time in weeks he was thinking of something other than fried egg sandwiches.

****

"OK," he said. "I'll help. But it won't be easy. Those dinosaurs are clever, especially the one with the horn."

They talked long into the night.
Outside the moon climbed up in
the sky. Its pale light shone down onto
Grubbler's house – and onto the other thing
that was there, the rusty machine towering
above the rooftop.

A gust of wind blew, and the metal hook
swung lazily on the end of its chain.

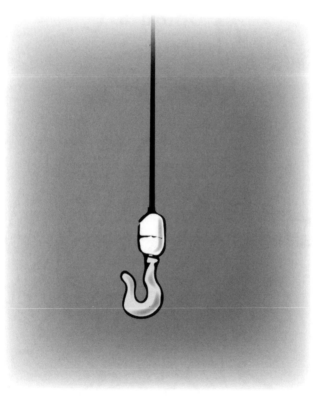

Chapter Two

. . . .

A Very
Promising Day

Grubbler was right, Protos was clever. The old Centrosaurus spent lots of his time thinking (he looked out of the window a lot) and reading. He liked talking to people too. He could answer most questions about dinosaurs. And when he couldn't, he would go straight to his Book Room at the city museum where he lived to look the answer up. But that wasn't what was most special about him.

If you asked Marlin Maxton (the boy who saved the Dinoteks) he would tell you: the *best* thing about Protos was that he was very gentle and very kind.

When Marlin arrived at the museum, on the first day of the school holidays, he found Comp and Siggy playing in the corridor.

The two little Troodons were chasing each other's tails and seeing who could jump the highest.

As soon as they saw Marlin they came running over to him. Their claws clattered on the stone tiles.

"Wait a minute!" Marlin laughed, as they raced around him in circles. "I'm getting dizzy! Do you know where Protos is?"

"He's in the garden," replied Siggy (still running). "He's with Little Dragon trying to cheer him up."

"Cheer him up? Why?"

They stopped.

Siggy lowered his voice gravely.

"Little Dragon thinks he's too small to be

a proper Dinotek."

"Yes," nodded Comp.

"Poor little thing."

"Oh dear," said Marlin. "That's not true, of course he's a proper Dinotek."

"Oh yes," agreed Siggy – but then he added: "He is very small though, isn't he?"

****

The garden was a peaceful place at the back of the museum, tucked away behind a moss-covered brick wall. There was a stream running through it and Marlin found Protos standing there with Little Dragon, the Meganeura, perched beside him on a rock.

Uncle Gus was there too and the old man turned and smiled.

19

"Hello lad!" he beamed. "You're just in time, look."

Marlin came over to see what was happening.

"You see?" Protos was saying. "It's just like I told you…"

The old creature was pointing at something. Little Dragon's head nodded and his wings buzzed.

"What is it?" asked Marlin.

The Meganeura took off and whizzed around them in excited circles.

"It's a very special moment," beamed Protos. "A new dragonfly is hatching."

They all looked.

There, on a reed sticking out of the stream, a most amazing thing was happening. A dragonfly (not a mechanical one but a real one) was emerging from its old skin, just like a butterfly coming out of a chrysalis.

"Up until this moment this creature has lived its whole life under water," whispered Protos. "But now it is becoming something different."

The dragonfly's new wings were stretching

out in the warm sun, drying, getting ready to
fly for the first time.

Little Dragon stretched his own wings out
too so that his solar batteries could soak up

energy from the sun.

Then suddenly the real dragonfly took off. It shot away, like a blue dart, along the stream.

Little Dragon whizzed after it.

"Not too close," called Protos. "Don't frighten it!"

So Little Dragon landed again and perched on his rock, watching as the dragonfly flitted up and down the stream, exploring its new territory.

Protos nodded, satisfied.

"There, I expect he'll stay here all day now."

"Yes I reckon he will," agreed Uncle Gus – then suddenly he looked at Marlin and clapped his hand to his head.

"But I nearly forgot! We've got something important to show you lad! Come on, come this way..."

Chapter Three

••••••••••••••••

More Dinoteks!

Uncle Gus led the way. They climbed up a stairway, through a hidden corridor at the back of the museum, and found their way to the Book Room.

There were more dinosaur books in that special place than in all the libraries of the world. Over the last few weeks Protos had been busy sorting through them all, putting them back into order.

"Come here lad," whispered Uncle Gus. "Look at this."

And he pointed to a cardboard box that was sitting on the floor beside a reading table. The box was tatty and beaten-up. Its bulging sides had been wrapped around with tape to stop them splitting open.

"What is it?"

Marlin knelt down to look.

"Something you found?" he asked Protos.

"No, not me. Police Inspector Bailey."

"She found it in the City Library," beamed Uncle Gus.

And they watched as Marlin lifted the flap and peeped inside.

There was a pile of papers – loose pages, notebooks and folders. The sheet on top had a picture of a dinosaur – an Ankylosaurus? – skilfully drawn in pencil.

"You'll never believe it," exclaimed Uncle Gus. "These are my old notebooks! My lost drawings and plans. Somebody must have taken them to the library all those years ago after I lost my memory. They've been sitting in there ever since, gathering dust."

He reached in and picked up one of the books.

"It's amazing stuff," he said, flicking it open. "I can't remember doing most of it!

Sauropods will need strong supporting frames – a design challenge but nature provides the answer!

for the T-Rex

Brachiosauru Dinotek (arm lizard)

Long, strong spine tail balances neck – like a cantilever bridge

Ankylosaurus

But look, these are all my plans for making Dinoteks."

Protos nodded.

"Yes, your uncle was getting ready to make more creatures like us."

"More Dinoteks?!" exclaimed Marlin

Uncle Gus nodded.

"'The designs are all here lad! They're just waiting to be built and brought to life…"

Brand new dinoteks – lots of them! This was the most exciting discovery Marlin could ever have dreamed of.

"Let's get started," said Uncle Gus, rolling up his sleeves.

"Yes!" cheered Marlin.

First, they laid the pages out on the floor and tried to work out which sheets belonged together, like piecing together the world's most exciting jigsaw.

There were so many pages they filled up the Book Room then went out, all the way along the corridor, and up the stairs.

There were lots of sketches of Ankylosaurus parts. Marlin ran back and forwards collecting them and handing them to Protos.

But that was just the start. There was an Oviraptor, an Iguanadon, a Styracosaurus and (Marlin was most excited to find) an Allosaurus.

"I can't wait to start building!" he said.

****

L ater that morning Marlin went to check on the other Dinoteks in the Forgotten Room. They were busy, practising for the museum's Spectacular Dinosaur Show.

"What do think, Marlin?"

growled Flame. The T-Rex was standing on top of a broken tree (which he'd just knocked over) holding Comp in his jaws.

"It looks very exciting," said Marlin.

"Don't worry," squeaked Comp. "It's

pretend. He's not really going to eat me!"

"But it's not too scary is it?" cawed Dacky, the Pterosaur, flapping his wings. "We don't want to frighten the children."

"They won't be frightened," said Marlin. "They'll love it."

****

After that he ran down to check that everything was OK in the ticket office.

The Office Manager, Susie Oxford, waved and smiled at him.

"It's all good," she beamed.

There were lots of visitors queuing up to get in (many more than in the old days when a certain grumpy person had been in charge).

Once or twice Marlin peeped out into the garden and saw Little Dragon sitting happily on his rock in the sun.

****

Everything was perfect. Then just before closing time something strange happened.

Chapter Four

∙∙∙∙∙∙∙∙∙∙∙∙∙∙∙∙

The Yellow Clue

Just before six o'clock, when the museum was about to close, Marlin noticed a woman standing outside the Dinosaur Gallery. There was something odd about her.

She was standing completely still and scowling. Her fingers were covered with gold rings.

Suddenly she came to life. She pulled a notebook from her pocket – it was bright yellow – and began jotting things down.

Her pen jabbed furiously at the paper.

"Yes, yes… just as I feared…" she muttered under her breath.

Marlin was about to ask her if she needed any help but at that moment she turned and walked away.

What was she writing?

Marlin followed her.

As she was leaving, striding down the museum steps, she dropped something.

A piece of bright yellow paper fluttered away.

"Look out…" Marlin called to her but she didn't hear him.

The yellow paper was caught by the wind and it went sailing upwards, round and round, and away over the museum roof.

Where it went after that, Marlin didn't see.

****

In bed that night Marlin lay awake thinking about Uncle Gus's amazing drawings. *More Dinoteks!* And the dragonfly flitting along the river. And the Dinoteks rehearsing their show.

Then his eyes closed and he thought about the strange woman and the little piece of paper, spinning away into the sky. Round and round, higher and higher…

He drifted off to sleep.

And the next thing he knew, something was tapping on his bedroom window.

****

"**D**acky? What are you doing here?"
The Pterosaur was standing right below his window, looking up. Moonlight shone silver on his wings.

"I need to talk to you boy," he cawed.

"But it's late!"

"I know," said Dacky, looking around. "I didn't know who else to tell."

Marlin nodded.

"OK. Wait a minute, I'll come down."

He crept to the back door as quietly as he could. He didn't want to wake his parents.

****

"**I** found this," whispered Dacky. "Up on the museum roof."

And he held up one of his claws. Clutched between two of the talons was a crumpled piece of paper.

"I'm not much good at reading boy, not like Protos. But I think it might be important."

Marlin blinked. The paper was bright yellow.

"Let me see."

He took it and stepped back into the light of the kitchen.

He rubbed his eyes and began reading. And suddenly he was wide awake.

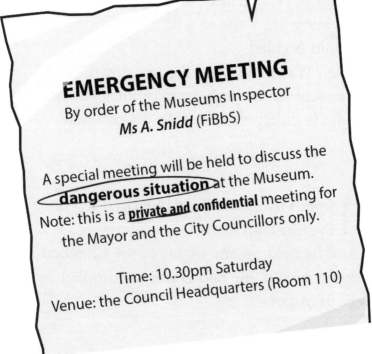

EMERGENCY MEETING

By order of the Museums Inspector
Ms A. Snidd (FiBbS)

A special meeting will be held to discuss the dangerous situation at the Museum.
Note: this is a **private and confidential** meeting for the Mayor and the City Councillors only.

Time: 10.30pm Saturday
Venue: the Council Headquarters (Room 110)

"Was I right?" cawed Dacky. "*Is* it important?"

"I...I think it might be," frowned Marlin.

The strange woman. This must be the note she'd dropped.

"We need to find my uncle," he decided – but then he glanced up at the kitchen clock. It was 10.20 already. According to the secret note the meeting was due to start at 10.30. He looked back at Dacky and thought for a moment.

Ten minutes...maybe a bit less...

Then he made up his mind.

"Do you remember the glass tower? Do you remember how to get there?"

****

Two minutes later they were swooping across the city, Marlin swinging in Dacky's claws.

"Hurry Dacky!" he shouted.

He looked up at the creature's wings, stretched out above him like a vast kite. The fabric billowed as the wind rushed over it.

"Don't worry boy! Hah! We'll be early!"

All at once they were going very fast. Marlin looked down and felt a sudden thrill. Beneath his dangling feet – *a long way beneath!* – the roads and buildings were sweeping past in a blur.

"Aaaak! Aaaak!"

Dacky banked sharply, then dived. Marlin's stomach lurched as they dropped straight down towards the tower.

Chapter Five

•••••••••••••••

A Good Place to Listen

There wasn't much time. Marlin sprinted across the roof and Dacky watched as he pulled at the door, testing whether it was locked.

The door opened.

Marlin glanced back.

"Wait for me here," he whispered.

Dacky nodded.

"Be careful boy!"

"I will," replied Marlin.

It seemed a crazy idea, coming here in the middle of the night. But Marlin did know this building, and he knew that spying might the only way to find out what was going on.

The stairs led downwards (the same stairs that Marlin had once sprinted up, escaping from Grubbler).

He crept down them now, as quietly as he could.

When he reached the bottom, he pressed his ear to the door, checking whether anybody was on the other side.

Silence.

Marlin pushed at the door.

Locked!

What now?

****

He ran back to the top of the stairs. Then he spotted something he hadn't noticed before.

There was another small door there, with a sign on it saying 'SERVICE ROOM'.

He pushed it open and found himself in a room full of machinery, cables, pipes and boxes.

A machine was whirring in the corner and lights blinked on and off.

Marlin was about to leave again when he heard something – it sounded like voices, a long way off, but clear.

Where was it coming from?

He followed the sound… and discovered a metal grille close to the floor. The voices seemed to be coming from inside it.

The meeting room must be just below him, and the sound was coming along a pipe.

Marlin tugged at the grille.

Maybe he'd be able to hear the voices better if… yes! The grille came off. And now he could see inside.

On the other side of the grille was a long, square-sided metal pipe – a duct.

The duct was quite wide and it sloped gently downwards.

Marlin leaned into it, and heard the voices more clearly.

"…thank you for…everyone…most important…emergency…dinosaurs…"

Dinosaurs! Marlin still couldn't quite hear everything but he knew he'd found it – this was definitely the right place!

Ahead, and just below, he could see a light shining into the dark tunnel. The light was coming from another grille at the other end – an opening into the meeting room below.

Quickly, he pulled a notebook and pencil from his pocket and let himself slide down into the pipe, until just his feet were left sticking out at the top.

He pressed his face up to the second grille, and peered down – down onto the polished table and comfortable chairs where the City Councillors were gathered.

Their meeting had begun.

Chapter Six

• • • • • • • • • • • • • • • •

The Problem Pencil

Arangula Snidd was very important, Marlin could tell that straight away.

It wasn't just because she was dressed very smartly, it was also because she didn't smile much.

She spoke with a stern look on her face and pointed at her notebook.

It was bright yellow.

All the people around the table listened and nodded.

"…yes, yes, that's quite right…" the Mayor said, sipping at his tea. "That's a good point."

"Thank you Mr Mayor. Now, if I may just show you my Emergency

Report…"

Emergency report…

Marlin pressed his ear to the metal grille, trying to make sense of it.

He scribbled down as much as he could in his notebook.

Ms Snidd was a Museums Inspector (… *Museums Inspector…*) and she toured the country, visiting museums everywhere to check on them (*everywhere… check on them…*) to make sure they were complying with safety regulations (…*something… safety… something…*)

Marlin kept writing. He hoped Uncle Gus would be able to make sense of it.

"Of course sometimes we have to close museums down, if we find serious problems…"

He understood what *that* meant, and he didn't like the sound of it.

And then the Mayor said something – something that made Marlin freeze.

"I've read your report Ms Snidd and it says something odd…it says…you think the Dinoteks could be *dangerous*?"

"Yes. I certainly do."

"But really... what makes you say that?"

"It's obvious. Nobody knows what's inside them. How do the creatures work exactly? Where do they get their energy from?"

"Well I er... I haven't really thought about it... but the Dinoteks have never hurt anybody – "

Arangula Snidd interrupted him and her voice sounded cross, like a teacher talking to a naughty child.

"Mr Mayor, you need to take this seriously! We must get answers!"

"We must?"

"Yes! If not, the whole museum will have to be shut down."

"Shut...shut down?"

She nodded.

"Closed Mr Mayor. The doors will be chained up and nobody will be allowed in – or out."

Marlin gasped – and dropped his pencil.

It slipped through one of the holes in the grille and spun down – PLOP! – into Arangula Snidd's tea.

For a moment nothing happened.

Snidd stared down at the pencil, goggle-eyed.

It was sticking out of her drink like the mast of a sinking ship.

"What…how…?"

And then she looked up – straight at the grille where Marlin was hiding.

"Hello?" she called. "Is somebody up there?!"

****

Marlin was stuck! He tried to move but he couldn't.

In the meeting room below everybody was jumping out of their chairs – heading for the door – but he was wedged tight.

He tried wriggling backwards – and maybe if he hadn't been in a panic, he would have managed it.

But instead he kept slipping.

Then, without warning, he felt strong hands grabbing hold of his feet and pulling him upwards, back out of the duct.

Buster Crank was delighted! He was grinning from ear to ear.

He'd spent years working as a security guard, but in all that time he had never caught a single criminal.

Until tonight.

"Up you come criminal!" he said. "Come to Buster!"

He pulled at the two feet and dragged the criminal upwards, out of the pipe.

"There! Got you!"

The criminal was quite small and light – Buster had hoped for something a bit bigger – but never mind, he had still made his very first catch…

And then he saw who it was.

"You!" he exclaimed.

Chapter Seven

．．．．．．．．．．．．．．．．

The New
Dinosaur Fan

Uncle Gus and Protos had stayed up all night working.

Now, as the morning light came sparkling in, Protos was looking at a picture of a Sauropod.

"Very odd..." he said thoughtfully. "Professor, you wrote *'finished'* on this one. I wonder why?"

"It must be because I'd finished the picture," Uncle Gus replied.

"I suppose so, but..."

And at that moment the sound of heavy footsteps came echoing along the passage towards them.

They looked up and a big man in a uniform appeared at the door.

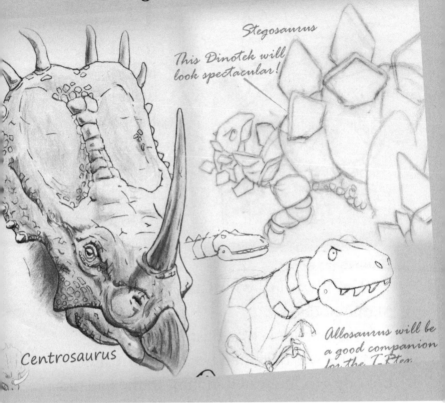

Dinotek designs and notes *A.A. Cogwell*

Stegosaurus

This Dinotek will look spectacular!

Centrosaurus

Allosaurus will be a good companion for the T-Rex.

It was Buster Crank.

"I've brought them back," the guard announced.

"Good, thank you," nodded Uncle Gus. Then he frowned. "Er, brought *who* back exactly?"

Marlin came in with Dacky, grinning. "Us!"

Everyone gathered round to hear what had happened.

"It was a close thing," cawed Dacky. "The boy nearly got caught."

"Yes, it was lucky Mr Crank found me," Marlin nodded.

Everyone looked at Buster.

Buster was delighted because normally nobody was interested in him. In the bad old days, when he worked for Grubbler, he just used to get shouted at a lot and told how stupid he was.

In those days the only thing Buster had to look forward to was eating sausages.

But not any more. Now Buster's life was good. He had discovered something new and fantastic. He had found out that he really loved dinosaurs.

He was mad about
them. He had even
started reading books
(well, *one* book so
far), and visiting the
museum. That's how
he had become Marlin's
friend.

"Tell us!" squeaked Siggy. "What
happened Buster Crab?"

"Not Crab, it's *Crank*," corrected Dacky.

"Tell us Crank!" squeaked Siggy.

"Well, it was like this…" began Buster,
and his eyes grew wide as he told the story
of how he'd cleverly spotted the burglar on
his security camera and gone up in the lift to
investigate.

"And guess what I discovered? It wasn't a
burglar at all."

"Really?! Who was it?!" squeaked Comp.

"It was Marlin, silly," snapped Dacky.

"Yes, Mr Crank got me out just in time,"
nodded Marlin. "Just before Miss Snidd
came in."

"Snidd?!" growled Flame. "Who's she?"

And then Marlin told them.

****

Everyone listened in silence as Marlin revealed what he'd discovered – about the secret meeting with the Mayor in the glass tower and Arangula Snidd's threats.

"She says she wants answers – and if she doesn't get them she'll close down the museum!"

Steg's armour plates rattled, and his lights flashed.

"But she can't do that. Can she?"

The Dinoteks looked at Marlin.

Marlin looked at Uncle Gus.

Uncle Gus was deep in thought.

"This is very odd," he frowned. "Very odd indeed. I didn't even realise there was such a thing as a Museums Inspector…"

And he ran a hand through his wild hair.

Protos stepped forward.

"Don't worry," the old creature said. "If she visits I'm sure she'll like us. She'll see at once that we're not dangerous."

******

Arangula Snidd *was* going to visit, and soon. She standing in the lobby at the council headquarters, waiting for the Mayor. In a few minutes she would be riding in his official black car to the museum.

An unpleasant grin spread across her face.

Her plan was working perfectly.

Now for the next step. Now to get the boy and the Professor away from the museum.

Snidd glanced around to make sure nobody was watching her. The lobby was deserted.

Good…

She pulled out her phone.

"Grubbler?" she whispered. "Are you in place? Excellent, keep hidden until I call. I'll deal with the Professor and the boy – after that, it's up to you!"

Suddenly the lift door hissed open and she stuffed the phone into her pocket as the

Mayor appeared.

"Ms Snidd. Are you…er, ready?"

"Yes," she replied. "I am."

Chapter Eight

•••••••••••••••••

The Inspection

The Mayor and Arangula Snidd arrived at the museum just as the bell in the clock-tower struck five.

Five chimes echoed across the square and on the steps far below Professor Cogwell was waiting.

Marlin watched from inside as Snidd approached. Her yellow notebook was ready in her hand.

"Hello!" beamed Uncle Gus. "I expect you've come to visit the museum? Welcome! We have a lovely new display of tropical insects and our collection of tractor wheels has just been cleaned up. Would you like to see them?"

The Mayor pulled out a tissue and

mopped his brow.

"Well, er…no. I…I have some bad news I'm afraid…"

"Oh dear," replied Uncle Gus. "You're not ill are you? Is it your stomach?"

The Mayor shook his head.

"No, no, not this time…but there have been some concerns…some er worries… about the Dinoteks…"

Before the Mayor could say any more Snidd butted in.

"Professor Cogwell, I am the National Inspector of Museums," she thrust out her hand for him to shake. "I'm here for a safety check."

"I see," replied Uncle Gus. "Well don't worry because everything is quite safe."

"Is it? I think that's for me to decide," she snapped. "I want to know how the Dinoteks get their power. I need to see everthing. *I need to see how it all works.*"

Uncle Gus scratched his head.

"Well I, er… follow me then and I'll show you…"

He led them into the museum.

Marlin followed, not getting too close. The Dinoteks crowded after him as quietly as they could.

The more Marlin saw of Arangula Snidd the less he liked her.

Maybe it was the way she kept looking at things, out of the side of her eyes, when she thought nobody was watching.

The Mayor didn't seem to have noticed. And nor had Uncle Gus.

They went into the workshop. There, beside a bench covered with tools, was a large cabinet made of wood and glass. Its front was a confusion of dials and levers. Uncle Gus pointed at it.

"This is it," he said. "This is the Dinotek Power Machine."

****

Not far away, at that very moment, Oliver Grubbler was waiting in the dark. He was squashed into a tight place and he was feeling just a bit uncomfortable.

He only had himself to blame of course. The truth is, if he hadn't spent the last ten weeks eating so many egg sandwiches things wouldn't be so tight for him right now.

He grunted and tried to turn over. Something ripped. Was that his trousers?

Never mind. He had other things to think about.

"Come on…come on…"

He stared at his phone, willing it to ring.

He couldn't wait! Because when that phone rang he would be going into action.

He sniggered.

Grubbler the Scruffy Pyjama Man was gone – Grubbler the Beast Slayer was back!

Chapter Nine

• • • • • • • • • • • • • •

The First Battle

"How does it work?" demanded Arangula Snidd.

"Oh it's not complicated," replied Uncle Gus. "You press a few buttons and turn a few knobs."

He waved his hand at the machine as if that explained everything completely.

Snidd leaned forwards. Her eyes scanned across the machine, studying it. Her pen hovered over her yellow notebook.

"But where does all the power come from?" she asked.

"Ahh," replied Uncle Gus. "That comes from inside. You see there's a –"

"Show me. Open it up."

Uncle Gus blinked.

"Actually I don't think that's a good idea. You see…"

"Professor! I need to see inside. If you don't show me I won't be able to write my safety report."

She tapped on the machine's glass front with her pen.

Marlin clenched his fists.

"No!" he almost shouted – but stopped himself just in time.

"OK," shrugged Uncle Gus. "But I've never done this before. I'm not sure what might happen…"

Marlin held his breath as the old man fished something out of his pocket – a little key – and reached out towards the cabinet.

"Here goes…" he sighed.

The door opened and everybody gasped. At once the room was flooded with a magical light. It was like the glow of a bonfire on an autumn night, sparkling gold and red.

There, inside the Dinotek Power Machine was a tangle of wires and wheels.

And in the middle of it all was a metal ball.

Light was shining out from it, glowing on their faces and dancing in their eyes.

Snidd stared at the ball greedily. The Mayor gawped, astonished. The Dinoteks gazed on in wonder.

It was as if everybody was under a spell.

"What...what *is* it?" gasped Marlin, forgetting to keep quiet.

"It's the Energy Orb," whispered Uncle Gus.

"This is what gives us all life," said Protos.

The old creature stepped forwards and lowered his horn.

"It needs to stay hidden away safely," he said.

And very gently, he nudged the door shut.

The golden-red light faded, and the spell was broken.

"Have you...er, have you seen enough Ms Snidd?" asked the Mayor, mopping his brow.

Snidd stood frozen for a second – then she shook herself awake.

"What?! Er, yes! That's enough for now."

She snapped her notebook shut.

"We can go," she said. "Oh! But there's just one more thing…"

She looked at Uncle Gus.

"I need you to come with me, back to the Council Headquarters to answer a few questions. And the boy."

She pointed at Marlin.

"Both of us?" said Uncle Gus. "Now?"

"Yes now. There are some forms you need to fill in. It won't take long."

Marlin noticed it again – that crafty look in her eyes – she was lying, he knew it!

"I can't come," he blurted out. "I'm busy!"

Snidd looked straight at him now – and there was a glint in her eyes, almost as if she had been hoping that he would argue.

"Too busy are you? Too busy young man? Well, I'd like to ask you about *this*…"

And she held up something in her hand for everyone to see. It was the pencil that he'd dropped into her tea!

"It seems that there was a criminal spying

on our our meeting last night. Wasn't there Mr Mayor?"

"Oh…er yes, a spy…"

"And whoever it was threw this pencil at me. A savage attack! Have you seen it before young man? Is this pencil *yours*?"

And she fixed him with a fierce stare. It was a commanding look, like the glare of a predator, warning him not to fight back.

It almost worked on Marlin (just as it had worked on Grubbler and the Mayor).

"Well?! Speak up!" she snapped, and Marlin felt himself beginning to blush.

But then he discovered something new about himself. He was actually quite tough, for a boy of his age.

He would never *dare* to argue if a teacher told him off. Or his parents.

But this was different.

Snidd was an enemy, he was sure of it. He looked straight at her and smiled politely.

"You are right," he said. "I did have a pencil just like that. But I dropped it on my way home last night. Somebody else must have found it."

It was such an outrageous lie that for

a moment Arangula Snidd was totally speechless.

"Oh, er…yes…" nodded the Mayor. "That happened to me once too… I'm always dropping pencils…"

Snidd looked furious but the Mayor continued.

"I, er… hate losing pencils like that. But at least you found it for him, eh?"

And he took it from her hand and passed it back to Marlin.

"Thank you," said Marlin extra politely. "I'm so glad to get it back. It's my favourite."

"That's all sorted then," nodded the Professor. "I'll come. The lad can stay here."

****

Marlin watched Uncle Gus leave with the Mayor and Arangula Snidd. Then he hurried back up to the workshop and found Protos still looking at the Power Machine.

"Do you think it was damaged?"

"No I don't think so," replied Protos.

But Marlin thought he didn't sound too sure.

Chapter Ten

• • • • • • • • • • • • • • • •

A Short Sleep and
a Strange Dream

Soon the museum was closed. All
the visitors went home but Marlin
stayed. He called his mum and told her
what had happened.

"Can I stay and look after the
Dinoteks?"

"OK," she replied. "Be good young
man. And make sure your friends
don't get into trouble. Especially those
little ones."

"Thanks mum!"

The Dinoteks waited to hear if
Marlin could stay – and they cheered
when he told them yes.

"Has the Horrible Snidd gone away

forever?" asked Siggy.

"When is the Professor coming back?" demanded Comp.

"I don't know," admitted Marlin.

"Soon," said Protos. "I'm sure he'll be back soon. And now we all need to get some rest. It's been a long day and everybody must be tired."

"But can't we play for a bit?" yawned Comp.

Dacky prodded him with his beak.

"No."

****

They huddled in a circle.

The Troodons curled up together, Dacky folded his wings and tucked his beak inside so that only his eyes were peeping out. Steg lay with his tail stretched out and his chin resting on his front paws. And Marlin found some cushions to lie on. He propped them up against Flame, and felt the big creature's motors purring deep inside.

He didn't say anything but he was still

worrying about Uncle Gus. What was Snidd up to? If only he could work it out…

He was still thinking about it as his eyes closed and he fell asleep too.

****

The museum was dark, nothing moved. Suddenly Marlin woke up. It was the middle of the night.

In the darkness he saw Protos standing beside the Power Machine. The old creature was frowning.

"Marlin? Are you awake?" Protos whispered.

"Yes," answered Marlin. "What's wrong?"

The Centrosuarus looked at him.

"I had a dream," he said. "I dreamed that somebody was calling to me from a long way off. They were lost and needed my help. "

"Calling to you? Who was it?"

"A lost Dinotek."

Marlin sat up and rubbed his eyes.

"But Protos… there *aren't* any other Dinoteks."

Protos nodded.

"That's what I thought too… but what if… what if there was another Dinotek that we'd all forgotten about? Like the ones in the Professor's drawings?"

The old creature looked at the Power Machine – and it seemed to Marlin almost as if Protos was trying to speak to it.

"The dream was so real," he mused. "A lost friend calling for my help…"

Suddenly Marlin gasped.

"Protos, look!"

The front of the Machine was glowing!

"It's never done that before," blinked Protos.

"Maybe it's trying to tell us something," Marlin said.

Now an even stranger thing happened.

A cloud of tiny, fizzing stars like little

fireworks appeared.

"Hello," said Protos – and the stars grew brighter and floated towards him.

They hovered right in front of his beak. Then they drifted away towards the door.

"You want us to follow you? Right away?

Well don't go too fast then…"

Protos lumbered forwards and followed the little sparks out of the room.

Marlin jumped up to wake the others.

****

Flame shook his head.

"What is it? What's happening?"

"We need to go," said Marlin.

Steg was awake now too.

"Protos thinks there's a lost Dinotek," Marlin told them.

"OK," said Steg. "I'll wake the others."

His tail lights came on, gently glowing.

"Come on little ones," he whispered to the Troodons. "It looks like we're going on an adventure!"

Dacky woke and shook open his wings.

All the Dinoteks woke. They went in a line after Protos – through the museum galleries, and out through the front door.

Chapter Eleven

....

The Old
Stuffed Walrus

Something else strange happened in the museum that night. It happened not long after Marlin and the Dinoteks had left.

One of the model animals in the Mammal Gallery came to life. It was a stuffed animal – a walrus that looked a bit like a giant grey sausage.

It had been on display there for more than a hundred years and in all that time it had never once moved.

But it did now.

It wobbled on its stand, back and forward, then rolled onto the floor.

KERFLUMP!
CRACK!

One of its tusks snapped.

Then a fist pushed out through its middle – "NYARGH!" – and two beefy hands appeared and ripped open a hole.

Grubbler squeezed himself out from inside the stuffed creature. He stood up, covered in feathers, and shook himself off.

"Ugh! Disgusting!"

He'd been hiding inside it for hours and now his legs were stiff.

He gave the walrus a kick – he had never liked the ugly thing – then he stomped off through the museum.

The phone call had finally come from Snidd.

It was time for Grubbler the Beast Slayer to go into action!

****

Grubbler blundered around in the museum for a while, charging up and down the corridors and getting lost. But eventually he found what he was looking for: the precious thing that Snidd had described to him.

In one of the corridors he noticed a strange glow. It was a gentle golden light that had a wonderful, magical feel (but Grubbler didn't notice that) – he crept forwards and looked. His eyes shone coldly.

There was the machine in front of him – the one that Snidd had told him about on the phone.

"Aaaahhh…just like she said…"

He pulled a screwdriver from his pocket and went to work.

It reminded him of something similar that he had done many years ago, when he was young.

("That wasn't my fault," he muttered. "I never meant to break it…")

Now, he jammed the screwdriver roughly into the machine, and prized open the door.

"Grubbler's revenge!"

Chapter Twelve

•••••••••••••••

The Journey Out

Marlin and the Dinoteks followed Protos through the sleeping city.

The line of sparks fizzed along in front. They passed shops and tall buildings in the city centre and climbed up narrower roads lined with houses, gardens and parks.

"Look! That's my school," whispered Marlin to Flame.

The classroom lights were all out and the gates were locked for the holidays.

"Cool," grinned the T-Rex.

The little stars kept going.

"Will we find a new Dinotek?" whispered Siggy.

"I don't know," replied Marlin.

"But we're going to look, just in case."

Siggy blinked.

"But Marlin. Where do new Dinoteks *come* from?"

Comp ran up laughing.

"They just appear, silly!"

Marlin couldn't think of a better answer, so he didn't say anything.

****

Soon they left the city and were walking along country lanes.

Trees and hedges grew tall on either side and Marlin felt as if he was venturing into a dark, leafy tunnel.

Here the air smelled of grass, sweet flowers and damp earth.

The only light came from ahead – from the little stars and from Steg's tail.

They kept walking.

Then Marlin heard a sound in the distance, a gentle roar.

Flame sniffed at the air.

"What is it?" cawed Dacky. "It sounds like the wind!"

"I don't know…" rumbled the T-Rex.

"It's the sea," Marlin smiled at them.

And soon their feet – and their claws – were sinking into soft sand, dotted with long, tough grass.

Flame laughed. His great claws sunk into the sand and slipped a bit with each step.

"Dunes," exclaimed Marlin. "We must be at the beach!"

They walked on, until suddenly Steg called out.

"The sparks! They've gone! They just whizzed away out to sea!"

****

Marlin peered into the dark, towards the sound of the breaking waves, but there was nothing to see.

"What does it mean?" he frowned.

The Centrosaurus shook his head.

"I'm not sure. Maybe I was wrong. Or maybe it means we're getting close…"

Suddenly Siggy gave a big yawn.

"I'm tired," he squeaked.

"Me too," squeaked Comp.

And the two of them sat down, right there in the sand.

Protos looked at them.

"You've been walking all night," he said. "You've done very well."

The others agreed. It was time to get some sleep.

Protos stood for a little while, staring out towards the sea. Marlin watched him.

Where had the sparks gone, he wondered? And how was Uncle Gus getting on?

Chapter Thirteen

. . . .

News of Success

It was almost midnight when Arangula Snidd's phone rang.

"Well? Is that you?"

"Yes. Of course it is. And I've done the job."

A triumphant smile spread across Snidd's face.

"You got the Energy Orb? Excellent! Any sign of the creatures?"

"No. The stupid things have gone wandering off somewhere…ouch!"

"Grubbler?! Grubbler! What is it?"

"Nothing…nothing…just a bit of walrus tusk in my shoe…"

"Stop messing around and pay attention! Remember the plan! Go to the place I told you about – the warehouse by the shore."

"OK. The warehouse."

"Leave the Orb there. We'll meet tomorrow night and plan our next move."

"Fine. And what about the Professor?" She turned back to the meeting room. The door was closed but she lowered her voice, just in case.

"Don't worry," she whispered. "I'll keep him talking for a few more hours."

Chapter Fourteen

· · · · · · · · · · · · · · · ·

Beside the Sea

Marlin slept late. The afternoon sun was already shining down through the long dune grass when he finally sat up, yawning.

The Dinoteks had all gone – all except for Steg who was lying close by, still snoring, with something on his head.

Marlin blinked and looked at him.

Somebody had balanced a pile of sand on top of him, like a hat!

Then he heard voices.

He stood up and saw that Comp and Siggy were running around by water's edge with Flame. They were daring each other to touch the waves.

And Protos was there too, collecting together sea shells and pebbles.

And then there was a roar – YAHOOO!!! – and Steg went thundering past Marlin. He ran down the beach, shaking the sand off his head and jumped into the waves with such an enormous SPLASH! that it knocked the Troodons over.

****

Flame came striding over to Marlin.
"I got you this," he said – and he reached round and lifted a bag from his back.

Marlin looked inside – two apples, a fruit bun and a cheese roll!

"You do like cheese, don't you?" grunted the T-Rex.

"Yes!" laughed Marlin – he was starving! "But where did you find it?"

"Easy," he replied. He nodded back across the dunes. "There's a house over there. The owners were very nice."

Now Protos joined them.

"Are you ready to go on?"

"Yes I'm good," replied Marlin. "But what about the stars?

Protos shook his head.

"They haven't come back," he said. "But they brought us this far so maybe the rest is up to us."

And at exactly that moment Dacky appeared. The Pterosaur swooped down and landed on the sand in front of them.

"I've found it!" he gasped. "I've found the lost Dinotek!"

Everyone crowded round.

"Where?!" exclaimed Marlin.

"That way!" he turned and pointed along the shore. "There's a strange place along there, boy. Buildings. I was just flying over it and I saw a creature."

"What did it look like?" growled Flame.

"It's big," replied Dacky. "Massive. And it's got a long neck…"

Chapter Fifteen

· · · · · · · · · · · · · · · ·

The Strange Quay

The Dinoteks hurried along the beach and went up into the dunes again.

The sun was beginning to sink but the strange place that Dacky had spotted was just ahead.

There was a concrete platform sticking out into the sea – a jetty.

An old, tumble-down building – some sort of warehouse – stood near the jetty's end.

And there, out at the far end with its arm leaning over the water, was a huge, rusty crane.

Its great hook was swinging lazily on the end of a long chain.

****

Suddenly Flame laughed.

"It's not a Dinotek! It's a crane – that's what you saw Dacky. Look, it's moving in the wind."

"I…I'm sure it wasn't that," said Dacky.

"It's OK," said Marlin. "We'll go and look."

But Siggy backed away.

"I don't like that place," he whispered. "It's spooky."

Comp nodded.

Steg looked at Protos.

"I think we should be careful," he said.

"Don't worry," said Marlin. "Why don't I go up with Flame first?"

****

Flame moved fast with Marlin riding on his back.

In four quick strides he was down from the dunes and speeding along the open beach.

The wind tugged at Marlin's hair and the last of the sun glinted on Flame's golden skin.

There was a river ahead, flowing down to the sea – deep and dark – but Flame didn't stop.

He jumped across and leapt straight up onto the quayside.

Marlin grinned.

"Neat."

"Easy," said the Rex.

Marlin clambered down onto the concrete.

"Why don't you wait here?" he whispered. "I'll look about quietly."

"OK," nodded the Dinotek. "But be careful."

"I will," said Marlin. He wasn't afraid because he had the T-Rex with him – but still, there was something strange about this place and he wanted to be quick.

****

Marlin ignored the nearest shed and headed straight for the big warehouse.

He ducked behind a stack of old barrels, keeping low, and looked at the building.

It was already dusk but he could see that the building's green paintwork was peeling and one of its doors was hanging loose on a single, rusty hinge.

Marlin pushed at the door and peered inside.

For a moment he couldn't see anything. It was pitch black and it had that strange, seaside smell of old ropes, salt water and tar.

Then Marlin's eyes began to see again – and his heart jumped.

Right in front of him, right there, was a

big heap of metal. Not just metal – machine pieces! And some of the parts were clearly recognisable. A silver claw. A massive jaw. Sections of armoured skin.

Dinoteks parts! Had someone found them? Or stolen them from the museum…?

He was about to step forward to look more closely when he heard a sound above him – SWOOOSSSH! – and something in the darkness moved.

He stood frozen, looking up.

"Hello? Hello – is somebody there?"

Then the thing moved again.

Looming out of the darkness above appeared a huge metal head.

Marlin stepped back – he was looking straight up into the eyes of a Dinotek Sauropod.

Chapter Sixteen

. . . .

Alone
in the Dark

In the city Professor Cogwell was staring glumly out the window of the Council Headquarters.

He sighed and looked at the Mayor.

They had been stuck in the same meeting room for a whole day (and a whole night!) – drinking tea, reading documents, filling in forms – but mostly waiting for Arangula Snidd.

Whatever she was doing, Snidd seemed to be very busy.

She kept bringing in new piles of documents for them to look at.

Each time she came she dumped the papers in front of the Professor and swept out again muttering to herself.

"Living machines…this is not good… against all the rules…"

Professor Cogwell scratched his head and looked at the Mayor.

"This seems like a big waste of time," he shrugged. "Are you sure we have to do it?"

"Well…yes…" said the Mayor. "Paperwork must be completed. Forms must be filled in."

Uncle Gus held up the latest form – a thick pile of papers stapled together, full of silly questions.

"This one wants to know how many rivets each Dinotek has! I don't think I've ever counted…"

"Well," replied the Mayor. "Perhaps you er… perhaps you should have done…"

****

Outside in the corridor Snidd's phone rang.

She answered it, whispering.

"Yes… the silly fools are still here, still

doing as they are told, don't worry… both of them, yes. You're ready? Good, I'll leave now – we'll meet at the warehouse."

And without another word she snapped off her phone, hurried away down the corridor, and left the building.

As she went, she dumped her dark blue jacket on the floor.

She would never need it again.

Five minutes later, she was speeding through town on a motorbike, towards the harbour.

There, a super-fast speedboat was waiting to take her the rest of the way.

****

Marlin looked up at the Sauropod.

"What's your name?" he whispered.

The creature blinked at him, but still didn't speak.

"It's OK," continued Marlin. "I'm a friend."

He glanced over his shoulder – something had banged in the distance, falling over – was it the wind?

"I don't know if you can understand me," continued Marlin. "But we need to leave – it's not safe here."

And then the Sauropod spoke at last.

"I can't leave," it said. "The Owner says it's dangerous for me outside."

"The Owner?" asked Marlin. "Who's the Owner?"

"The Owner who made me," replied the creature.

"She said I have to stay in here and –" Then its head lifted up in alarm. The door nudged open and Flame appeared at the opening.

The Sauropod flinched backwards.

"Marlin, we should go," the T-Rex said. "There's a boat coming this way. I think – Oh! Hello there!"

He'd noticed the Sauropod.

"So we found you then," he grunted. "What's your name big one?"

"N…name?"

"Yes," said Flame. "What do people call you?"

"Nobody calls me anything," replied the

creature.

"That's useless," snorted Flame. "Never mind, we'll find you a name later. I'll just call you Friend for now."

And he turned back to Marlin.

"We should go," he said again.

****

The roar of the boat engine was still far off but now clear above the sound of the sea. And then Marlin heard something else too – more engines.

He glanced past Flame and saw lights moving along the shore, towards the jetty.

Flame was looking too.

"Cars!" he warned. "Or trucks. There must be a road out there…"

The T-Rex turned to Marlin.

"This could be a trap!"

And he growled, a low rumbling, warning sound from deep inside.

Marlin nodded – he had to think fast.

"Flame! See if you can block the road into this place. Keep them back, just for a few minutes."

"No problem," said the T-Rex. He turned and strode away into the dark.

Marlin looked back to the Sauropod.

"Will you come with us?" he coaxed. "I don't think the Owner made you really. I think it was someone else – I know him. He's a kind man. He's called the Professor."

"Pro…Professor…?" whispered the

Sauropod.

And suddenly a new look appeared on the great creature's face.

A look of hope.

"I… I remember that name…"

"Yes!" said Marlin. "And I'll take you to him – he'd love to see you!"

But then the creature's head dipped down again, towards its front leg – and now Marlin saw for the first time that a thick, rusty chain had been clamped around its foot.

"I am not allowed out."

"Of course you are! Everyone is!"

The sight of the chain filled Marlin with a sudden anger. He grabbed at it, dragging it frantically – but its thick iron links were too heavy for him to even lift.

He could hear the engines getting nearer.

"Pull!" he urged the Sauropod. "Try! You're strong! You can break it if you only try!"

But even as he spoke there was a crash outside and the warehouse was flooded with light. The doors burst open.

Marlin spun round.

And there was Protos.

The little stars had returned, and they fizzed and sparkled, filling the whole place. The Sauropod stared at them in wonder.

"It's time to go," said Protos.

And he lifted his front foot and stamped down on the chain. It shattered.

"Follow me," the old Dinotek said.

And he turned, and walked into the dark.

****

The Sauropod was huge.

Marlin could see for the first time just how big it was as it heaved itself forwards out of the warehouse and swayed along the jetty after Protos.

Its body was as long as all the other Dinoteks put together. Its tail swept slowly and gracefully from side to side. And its head now towered upwards into the sky.

Marlin was about to follow too when he noticed something.

The sparkling light of the little stars had faded again – the warehouse was dark once more – except for the pile of stolen Dinotek machine parts. That was still glowing.

Marlin went closer to look.

Why was it glowing?

And he gasped.

"How did… how did that get here?"

Tucked away behind one of the metal plates was a shining, silver ball.

It was the Energy Orb!

He grabbed it up and sprinted after the others.

Chapter Seventeen

· · · · · · · · · · · · · · ·

The Dinoteks
Retreat

Protos led the Sauropod down to the river.

"What… what is it?" the giant Dinotek asked, looking suspiciously at the dark water.

"Nothing to fear," said Protos.

He dived in and swam across with only his beak held up out of the water. At the far bank he scrambled and pulled himself out.

"It's quite easy," he called. "Come along."

After a moment's hesitation the Sauropod followed, stepping into the water.

Marlin looked back.

"Flame!" he shouted. "Quick! We can go now!"

He wondered whether the T-Rex had heard him – but a moment later the creature appeared out of the darkness, his eyes flashing.

"Marlin," he growled. "I've blocked the road with some wood, but I bet they'll clear it soon enough. There's a whole army of them coming."

Marlin gasped. A whole army!

"Come on. Let's get back to the dunes."

They ran – and they had hardly got out of sight before the whole area was flooded with light.

A speed boat came racing up

alongside the jetty in a shower of spray – and up above, on the quayside, the first of the trucks roared into view and screeched to a halt.

****

Grubbler stepped out of the truck. He waited.

The driver of the boat was already climbing up a ladder, stepping onto the jetty.

"Ah Grubbler, you are just in time. And you've met my people I see?"

Grubbler nodded.

Figures in yellow and black were climbing out of the trucks around him, scurrying about. Grubbler felt as if he were in a wasp's nest.

"Yes!" he smiled, rubbing his hands together. "It's quite a party!"

But Snidd was looking past him. She had spotted something – the line of fresh footprints leading up the bank on the other side of the river and disappearing into the darkness.

"No. It's not a party Grubbler," she said. "It's a hunt."

Chapter Eighteen

·················

The Way Back

"There's no time to talk," said Protos. "We must get home as quickly as we can."

Steg, the Troodons and Dacky were crowding round, staring up at the Sauropod in open amazement.

"You're so big…" gasped Comp. "Huge…Colossal…"

"Massive!" agreed Siggy. "And you'll never fit inside the museum."

"Shhh!" snapped Dacky. "Don't be rude!"

Then Flame came striding up and Marlin called out to Protos.

"Look! Somebody must have stolen it!"

He held up the Energy Orb.

The Dinoteks – including the Sauropod – all fell silent, staring at the shining ball in wonder. The light glowed on their metal faces.

But Protos shook his head.

"This is not good," he said. "The Orb should be back at the museum, back in its proper place."

Then he lowered his voice.

"Without it there, the Power Machine won't work. We'll run out of energy."

Siggy squeaked.

"I…I feel tired…"

"No you don't," said Dacky. "You're just imagining it."

"Maybe," said Protos. "But I'm afraid we'll all be feeling tired soon…"

The Pterosaur opened his wings.

"Let me go! I can fly back to the museum in a few minutes – and I know where the Orb goes."

"Brilliant," exclaimed Marlin. "That's the answer!"

Protos agreed.

"Yes, fly Dacky, as fast as you can!"

"Now it's time for us to go too," said Protos, as soon as Dacky had disappeared into the sky. Going fast now, he led the group down through the dunes and along beside the sea.

Marlin rode on Flame's back and the Sauropod followed close behind.

They walked on and soon it became clear that Siggy wasn't imagining it – he *was* feeling tired, and so was Comp.

The two little ones trudged beside Protos with their heads and tails drooping.

Until Siggy stumbled and fell.

Steg came hurrying over and scooped him up, lifting him onto the end of his spiked tail.

"Up you come," he said. "You too Comp, there's room for both of you."

They walked on.

"Can you manage?" whispered Protos.

"Yes," replied Steg. "They're not heavy."

But as they walked Marlin noticed that the Stegosaurus's lights were flickering and starting to go out.

****

"Look!" hissed Flame, staring backwards.

Marlin looked over his shoulder to see what the T-Rex was pointing at.

The moon was now rising behind them and in the distance the jetty stood out like a black strip, against the sea.

Lights were flashing and waving around by the warehouse, and he thought he could see little figures running about too – climbing down onto the beach.

But that's not what Flame was staring at.

It was the other thing – the crane that leaned out over the sea with its hook and chain. The crane wasn't at the end of the jetty any more. It was half way along it, moving towards the land.

"It's a good job we got away from that place," whispered Marlin.

"Yes," rumbled Flame. "But we left our footprints behind. A nice clear trail for enemies to follow."

And they turned and hurried after the others.

****

Dacky was alone now in the vast, night sky. He could hear the waves breaking below him and he could see, far off, a ship's light twinkling on the sea.

103

The wind was pushing him outwards, out over the water. But he turned against it.

He wheeled, and steered back in towards the land. Clear in the distance he could see the lights of the city. He knew that somewhere among all those lights was the museum.

Fly straight there. Don't wait. Don't stop…

He gripped the silver ball and beat his wings harder.

****

Marlin kept looking back. He was sure they were being followed.

But he knew the Dinoteks couldn't go any faster. They were walking in silence, using up all their strength.

Steg was stumbling now too.

"Let me help you," said Flame.

He leaned down and picked up the Troodons from Steg's tail, and carried them gently in his jaws.

Marlin climbed down from Flame's back

and jumped onto the sand – there was no point giving the T-Rex any extra weight to carry.

"You'll love the museum," Protos was telling the Sauropod. "There are so many rooms to look in. Some of them are small but of course you'll able to poke your head in through the windows. And we have lots of visitors who are interested in Sauropods."

"Is it…is it safe?"

"Safe? Of course it is! I do believe it's the safest place in the world."

The Sauropod plodded on, slower and slower.

******

Presently, Flame stopped and turned back to Marlin. He lowered his head and dropped the Troodons gently onto the sand.

"Steg is finished," he said quietly.

Marlin looked up and he saw the tail lights on the Stegosaur flicker one last time, then die. The great creature slumped down onto his knees, and froze.

Flame looked back along the dark shore.

"Hunters," he growled. "They're close."

Then Protos came lumbering over.

"I think we'll have to stop here," said the Centrosaurus.

"Yes," grunted Flame.

Protos looked at Marlin.

"You must leave us now," he said gently. "Don't be afraid. Just run fast and find a safe place to hide."

"No, I can't leave you!" Marlin exclaimed.

"You must."

Marlin looked up at Flame, tears pricking his eyes, but the T-Rex nodded.

"Protos is right."

And the Rex lowered his great head and nudged Marlin gently towards the dunes.

"Don't let them catch you. Use all your skill Marlin. I know you can do it."

Marlin stumbled away towards the dunes.

****

"Oh dear, I'm sorry Flame. I'm afraid I won't be able to help you much," said Protos. His head was drooping.

"It's OK," said Flame. "Don't worry."

And he looked up at the Sauropod.

"How are you feeling?" he asked.

"Like… like I'm dreaming," replied the giant. "But it's a good dream – because I'm not afraid any more."

"That's good," smiled the T-Rex – and he glanced at the figures now coming fast towards them.

They were spread out in a line, carrying long nets between them. And behind came the rusty crane on caterpillar tracks, lumbering towards them with its hook swinging like a heavy steel club.

"We have some rules, don't we Protos?" said Flame

"Rules…" Protos nodded, "Yes we do… very important…the Golden Rules…"

Flame continued.

"It means we never hurt anybody. But if we're attacked, we can fight back."

He looked up at the Sauropod.

"So if I had a nice long tail like you, the thing I'd probably do is whip up a lot of sand."

Flame smiled, and without another word – before the people with their nets and ropes could get any closer – he strode out to meet them.

He was tired, as tired as he'd ever been in his life, but at that moment he didn't look it. He stepped over the first line, and brushed away the net with an easy kick.

He headed for the crane.

More nets came, tangling around him, but he ignored them. He was watching out for the hook. It swung round out of the darkness, whistling through the air, aiming straight for his head.

****

Arangula Snidd roared in triumph. She was driving the crane across the sand and the T-Rex was right in front of her now.

"Got you!" she snarled.

The steel hook swung. Flame caught it in his teeth. He pulled hard, growling, and the chain snapped tight. The arm of the crane groaned – rusty flakes dropped off it – but it held. And then it pulled back.

Flame's feet began to slide and he felt his strength fading at last.

In that moment two thoughts passed through his mind.

He heard the WOOOSH-WHIP! of the Sauropod's tail, and felt waves of sand showering down on the beach.

The Sauropod had done well, he thought approvingly – yes, in the end, the timid creature had been surprisingly brave.

And the other thing he thought about was his friend Dacky.

He wondered if the Pterosaur had made it back to the museum yet.

Chapter Nineteen

. . . .

The Fall
of the Dinoteks

Dacky had never had such a hard flight. The wind was against him all the way and it was getting stronger.

Pterosaurs weren't made to fly like this. When the wind grew too strong they were supposed to find somewhere safe to shelter.

But Dacky knew that couldn't do that. He had to get to the museum.

He flew on – fighting, fighting. The Energy Orb glowed in his beak – as if it were trying to encourage him – but it was no use. Inside his chest he could feel his battery dying.

And then he saw the museum dome!

But his sharp eyes faded and he felt himself fall.

Down he dropped, tumbling and spinning.

And he crashed in a heap, one block away from the museum, in an overgrown garden.

The silver ball tumbled from his beak and dropped into a pile of leaves.

Nobody was there and nobody saw him fall.

****

The Dinoteks fell. On the beach Flame and the Sauropod lost their battle. The Troodons and Steg lay together in the sand. Protos stood with his head bowed.

And Dacky, in the garden so close to the museum – so close, but so far – lay lost and tangled.

All the Dinoteks fell.

Except for one. A blue-and-white flash suddenly shot out of the museum entrance. Little Dragon had spent whole the day in the garden, sleeping in the sun, and his solar batteries had soaked up its power.

Now he buzzed along the street like a speeding dart. He found his way to the garden and the pile of leaves and he dived into it. The silver ball was calling to him.

The little creature was not very strong, not at all. But he lifted the ball in his tiny legs and somehow flew with it just above the ground. And that's how he was flying – skimming over the grass – when he crashed into the Professor's leg.

Professor Cogwell had finally got fed up with filling in forms and had decided to go back to the museum.

"Little Dragon! Careful lad, mind your wings won't you – and what's that you've got…? Good grief! What are you doing with *that*…?!"

****

The net hunters finished tying Flame up. They wrapped his legs round and round with nets. And they put a thick rope around his jaws.

"Pull it tight!" ordered Snidd, climbing

113

down from the cabin of the crane.

Then she turned and shouted into the dark.

"Grubbler! We've done it. The plan worked."

It was her moment of triumph.

She raised her hand – "Pull!" – and the yellow-and-black figures got to work dragging the Dinoteks back along the beach.

By morning she'd have the creatures loaded onto a ship, ready to be carried away.

Snidd laughed.

"This is even better than I hoped. Not just a Sauropod, now I've got them *all!*"

But she was wrong.

At that very moment, back in the city, Little Dragon was watching as the Professor fixed the Power Machine.

*****

The T-Rex woke.

His head lifted and the net hunters jumped backwards, hanging onto the ropes.

But the ropes snapped and the nets tore.

And suddenly all the Dinoteks were waking around them.

Snidd jumped away from the crane (which was being pulled, crashing to the ground) and began to sprint across the sand, with the net hunters.

"The plan!" she shrieked. "This isn't in the plan! Everybody run!"

But it's hard to run in waterproofs.

Especially when there's a T-Rex coming after you.

Chapter Twenty

· · · · · · · · · · · · · · · ·

The Mayor
Learns Something
Important

It was past midnight. The city streets were empty and the moon shone down on the Museum.

The Mayor strode up the steps and hammered on the door.

"Professor? Professor Cogwell!"

For once his face wasn't grey, it was an angry pink.

The door opened and the Professor looked out.

"Ah, Mr Mayor. I thought it might be Marlin. You haven't seen the lad anywhere have you?"

But the Mayor ignored him.

"Professor, this is really not good enough! You didn't finish the paperwork."

Professor Cogwell sighed.

"It seems like such a waste of time…"

"Ms Snidd will not be happy," continued the Mayor. "Not happy at all…"

"No," said a voice. "She won't."

And they both turned.

"Ah, hello lad!" beamed the Professor. "Glad to see you back."

Marlin was striding across the square towards them. But the Mayor wasn't looking at him – he was staring at the creature following.

"Goodness!"

It was Flame, and dangling from his teeth was a sorry looking figure in yellow and black waterproofs.

"Ms Snidd!" gasped the Mayor. "Why are you dressed like that? Have you been sailing?"

"Not sailing, Mr Mayor," replied Marlin. "But she has been quite busy. "

And he told them everything that had happened.

As he listened the Mayor's mouth dropped open. He had never been more surprised in his life.*

****

It took a few days for the Museum to get back to normal.

Inspector Bailey came over from the police headquarters and took Ms Snidd away for questioning.

Uncle Gus made some improvements to the Dinotek Power Machine. Most importantly, he fixed the Energy Orb gently but securely so that nobody could ever take it again.

"I'm pleased everything has worked out so well," he beamed.

He was even more pleased (a hundred times more) the first time he saw the Sauropod. It came walking across the square with the others, looking around curiously, its tail waving gracefully, high above their heads.

Uncle Gus's eyes lit up. He pointed,

* Except for once, maybe – the time when he was chased by a giant mechanical spider (see Book 3).

119

speechless – and you could almost see his lost memories flooding back to him. It was like watching a thirsty plant being given water and seeing its leaves lifting up before your very eyes and its flowers opening.

"Good heavens! I remember you!" he exclaimed. "And how wonderful you look!"

The Sauropod smiled – it was the biggest smile ever seen on a Dinotek – and everyone cheered.

"But you still won't fit inside," squeaked Siggy.

****

S he did though.

A special sliding wall was built so she could get in and out (Buster Crank helped to make the hole for it – he came to the museum on his day off, carrying his favourite sledge hammer).

The Sauropod was too big to get upstairs to the Forgotten Room, but a special area was made for her near the entrance hall.

Flame waited very patiently for the

building work to be finished because he had something to say.

"Listen everybody!" he called.

He looked up at the Sauropod.

"It's time to decide what we should call our new friend."

"A name!" said Steg. "You must have a name!"

Everyone made a suggestion and some were quite good.

Siggy suggested 'Stomp'.

But Comp shook his head – 'Stomp' sounded too much like 'Comp'.

"How about Biggy?" he squeaked.

But Siggy didn't like that (for a similar reason).

Protos said that both 'Stomp' and 'Biggy' were very good names, but perhaps something like 'Heavy Lizard' would be better – because the Sauropod was a Barosaurus and that's what Barosaurus actually means.

"So it would be educational…"

But in the end it was Flame who came up with the best name.

"How about this," he asked, looking up at the Sauropod. "How about Sandy?"

Her face lit up and she laughed.

"Yes! I'd like to be called that."

And she flicked her tail, just like she had on the beach.

****

And after all that there was one Dinotek who got a special treat.

When all the work was over a special party was held to celebrate the heroic actions of Little Dragon.

The Meganeura buzzed around happily then landed on Protos's horn.

"You see," whispered the Centrosaurus. "Small creatures are just as important as big ones."

Chapter
Twenty One
· · · · · · · · · · · · · ·
The Missing
Pieces

Inspector Bailey finished questioning Arangula Snidd at the police station, and a few days later she called by to give Professor Cogwell and Marlin the news.

"There is enough evidence to send her to court. She will be put on trial for impersonating a public official."

"Pretending to be a Museum Inspector you mean?" asked Marlin.

"Exactly Marlin, pretending to be a Museum Inspector. It was a very clever act – and quite against the law. She'll be in serious trouble."

"Don't forget the stealing," said Uncle Gus. "She took the Energy Orb remember?"

But Inspector Bailey shook her head.

"I have my doubts about that Professor. I've studied your damaged walrus, and I agree that somebody was definitely hiding inside it. But from the size of the rip I would say that it wasn't Arangula Snidd. It was somebody much bigger."

"Grubbler!" said Marlin. "I bet it was him."

"I thought so too," agreed the Inspector. "So I paid him a visit. I asked Mr Grubbler what he was doing that night and he claims he was cleaning his house. I have to say, it did look rather spotless."

"I don't believe him," said Marlin.

"Actually, neither do I," she replied. "But I have no proof – yet."

She stood up to leave.

"I'll be keeping an eye on him though, don't worry."

At the door she stopped and turned back to them.

"Ah, I nearly forgot – what about

those Dinotek parts that Marlin found? They shouldn't be left lying around at the warehouse. Will you go and collect them?"

"Good heavens! I'd forgotten all about them!" exclaimed Uncle Gus. "It's time to get on with the important stuff – my lost designs… all those creatures! Where's Protos? We've got so much to do …"

He jumped up and began pacing around the room in his excitement. Marlin grinned.

"We'll definitely need to get those missing pieces uncle," he said.

"Good idea," said a voice. "Let's go – I feel like a run."

It was Flame, standing at the door.

****

The T-Rex raced with Marlin out to the old quay – and not just Marlin. Police Inspector Bailey came along for the ride.

They sped along the beach, and when they arrived the police officer's hair was ruffled and sticking up.

She was smiling broadly.

"Excellent," she nodded. "What a good way to travel."

Flame looked very pleased.

"If your car ever breaks, just come and find me."

Marlin was already heading over towards the warehouse. It looked the same as before – the peeling paint, the door hanging loose on its hinge – nothing had changed.

"Careful," called the Inspector.

She pulled a torch from her pocket.

"Let's just make sure it's safe…"

She crept forwards, shining the beam into the darkness. It revealed a large, empty space. Nearby was a jumble of ropes and boxes.

"Look! There's the chain!" hissed Marlin, pointing to the shattered iron links.

"Yes… and are those your stolen parts?"

The beam was now shining on the heap of metal pieces – claws, teeth, a club tail (Marlin knew what that was for) and armour plates.

"Yes, this is it," he whispered. "It's everything we need!"

****

Flame scooped the pieces up and dropped them onto his back.

"I won't be long," the T-Rex rumbled. "I'll take these home and come back for you."

"Good idea," said the Inspector.

She turned to Marlin.

"Shall we have a look along the jetty?"

So they did.

They walked out towards the very end of the platform and found a good spot to sit and wait. Out here it felt as if the rolling sea was all around them.

"Thanks for helping us again Inspector," said Marlin.

She smiled.

"Oh I'm just doing my job Marlin," she repied.

But then she added: "Between you and me though, I was very glad to help. I'm really looking forward to seeing all the new Dinoteks..."

The End
(but look out for Book 5!)

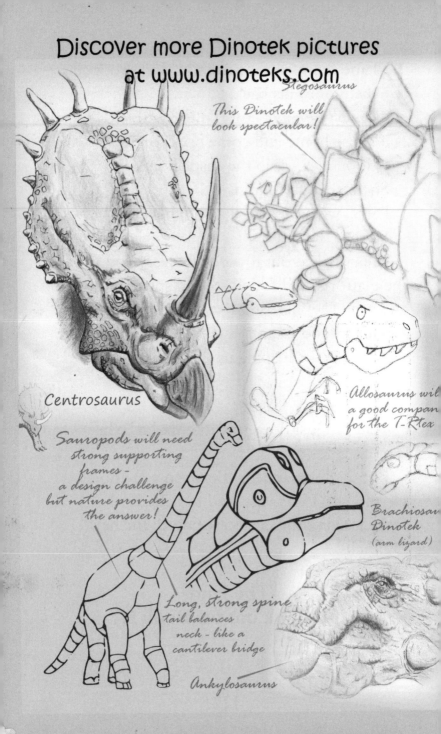

Discover more Dinotek pictures
at www.dinoteks.com

Stegosaurus

This Dinotek will look spectacular!

Centrosaurus

Allosaurus will a good compan for the T-Rtex

Sauropods will need strong supporting frames - a design challenge but nature provides the answer!

Brachiosau Dinotek (arm lizard)

Long, strong spine tail balances neck - like a cantilever bridge

Ankylosaurus